Penguin

MULAN
AND OTHER
TALES OF HEROES

LEVEL

RETOLD BY NICK BULLARD
ILLUSTRATED BY JIA LIU, POONAM MISTRY, AVIEL BASIL
AND LOUISE WARWICK
SERIES EDITOR: SORREL PITTS

PENGUIN BOOKS

UK | USA | Canada | Ireland | Australia
India | New Zealand | South Africa

Penguin Books is part of the Penguin Random House group of companies
whose addresses can be found at global.penguinrandomhouse.com.
www.penguin.co.uk   www.puffin.co.uk   www.ladybird.co.uk

Penguin
Random House
UK

Ladybird Tales of Superheroes first published by Ladybird Books Ltd, 2019
This Penguin Readers edition published by Penguin Books Ltd, 2021
001

Original text for "The Legend of Hua Mulan" written by Maisie Chan
Original text for "Hanuman, Demon Fighter" written by Sarwat Chadda
Original text for "Shahrazad the Storyteller" written by Sufiya Ahmed
Original text for "Anansi the Spider-Man" written by Yvonne Battle-Felton
Text for Penguin Readers edition adapted by Nick Bullard
Original copyright © Ladybird Books Ltd, 2019
Text copyright © Penguin Books Ltd, 2021

"The Legend of Hua Mulan" illustrated by Jia Liu
"Hanuman, Demon Fighter" illustrated by Poonam Mistry
"Shahrazad the Storyteller" illustrated by Aviel Basil
"Anansi the Spider-Man" illustrated by Louise Warwick
Illustrations copyright © Ladybird Books Ltd, 2019

Printed in China

The authorized representative in the EEA is Penguin Random House Ireland,
Morrison Chambers, 32 Nassau Street, Dublin D02 YH68

A CIP catalogue record for this book is available from the British Library

ISBN: 978-0-241-54377-1

All correspondence to:
Penguin Books
Penguin Random House Children's
One Embassy Gardens, 8 Viaduct Gardens
London SW11 7BW

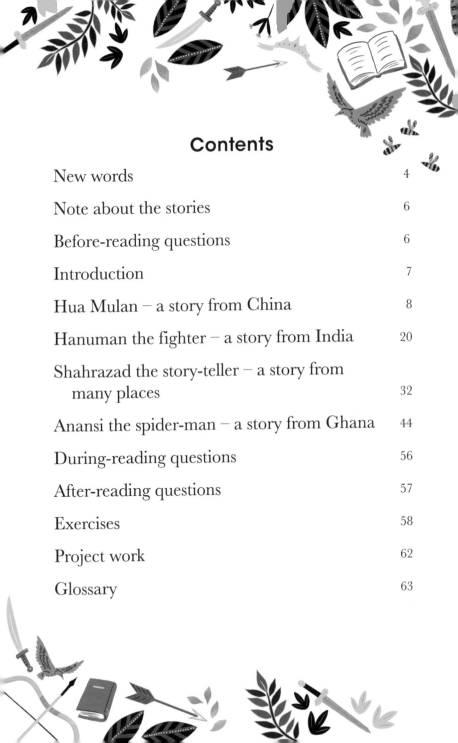

Contents

New words   4

Note about the stories   6

Before-reading questions   6

Introduction   7

Hua Mulan – a story from China   8

Hanuman the fighter – a story from India   20

Shahrazad the story-teller – a story from
   many places   32

Anansi the spider-man – a story from Ghana   44

During-reading questions   56

After-reading questions   57

Exercises   58

Project work   62

Glossary   63

New words

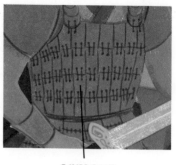

armour

demon

hornet

king

leopard

monkey

snake

soldier

spider

tail

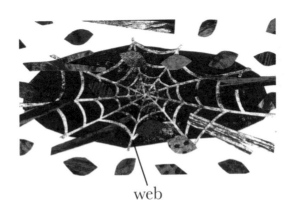

web

Note about the stories

Everybody loves stories. People across the world listen to and read them. The stories in this book are very old, and many of them are about special people or animals. These heroes can do very special things.

Many people have a favourite hero. Do you have a favourite? Why are they a hero? What special things can they do?

Before-reading questions

1 Look at the four names on the "Contents" page. Do you know any of these people? What do you know about them?

2 Did these people really live, do you think, or are they just stories?

3 These people were all heroes. They did some special things. Who are your heroes? What special things do/did they do?

Introduction

Every hero is very special. These are the stories for the four heroes in this book.

Hua Mulan comes from China, and many people know her from books and films. Someone first wrote about Mulan on paper in about 600 CE, but her story is older than that. Mulan's special **power*** is fighting.

Hanuman the monkey **god** comes from a long Indian story – the Ramayana. He is a very good friend to Rama. Hanuman's special power is changing from one thing to another. He is not always a monkey but he can be a man, or different animals. He is sometimes very big and sometimes very small.

Shahrazad's story comes from many countries, from India to Iran, Iraq and Egypt, and many people know her famous 1,001 stories. Shahrazad's special power is telling stories. She is **brave** and intelligent, and she likes to help other people.

Anansi comes from Ghana, and many people in that country tell stories about him. Anansi is often a spider and his special power is making spider webs. He is also very intelligent.

*Definitions of words in **bold** can be found in the glossary on pages 63–64.

Hua Mulan – a story from China

A very special girl lived in a village in China. This is her story.

After many years at **war**, a soldier came back home to his village. His name was Hua, and he put a young tree in his front garden. The tree grew tall, and after ten years there was a beautiful white and pink flower on it. That same year, Hua's wife had a baby girl. They gave the girl the name Mulan. That is the name of the beautiful flower in Chinese.

Mulan grew from a baby to a strong and brave young woman. She helped her mother in the house, but she loved to be with her father, too. She was wonderful with horses. She learned to fight, and she was very good with a sword.

"Fighting is important for you and your family, Mulan," said her father. "You're a girl, I know. But maybe you will need to fight one day."

One day, Mulan saw a lot of people in the middle of the village. There was a big notice there. The people read it, and they talked about it. Mulan read the notice, too.

"The king is going to war," she read. "One man from every house must be a soldier and he will fight for the king."

The names of a lot of men in the village were on the notice, and one name was Mulan's father. She was very sad. "My father was a fine soldier, but he's an old man now," she thought. "He can't fight. He can't go to war. He'll die before the first fight."

Mulan stopped for a minute. "But I'm young and strong," she thought, "and my father taught me well. I can fight with my eyes closed and with one hand behind my back. I'm good with a sword, and I can ride a horse very well."

Mulan talked to her younger sister. "I'll go to war for father. I can fight as well as a man."

"But father will not want you to go," said her sister.

張亦　花弧　趙常

劉起　李二文

"I'm not going to tell him," said Mulan. "It's a **secret**."

"But you're a girl!" said her sister. "People will see your long hair. And they'll see the pretty **make-up** on your face."

"It's OK," said Mulan. "I can change that."

Mulan put her long hair on the top of her head, and she took off all the make-up from her face. She took off her clothes. Then she wore her father's old armour, and she held his sword. Her sister watched. Mulan was now a different person.

"You're a man, now," said her sister.

"Yes," said Mulan. "But that's not important. Clothes tell you nothing. The important thing is inside me." She put her hand on her body. "Inside this armour there's a true soldier. But remember! It's a secret. Father must not know."

Mulan's little sister said goodbye to Mulan. "You'll come home a famous soldier. I know that," she told her.

Mulan took her best horse, and she rode away from the village. She met some men from other villages, and they all rode together. They crossed the great Yellow River, and they rode to the king's city.

In the city they met thousands of soldiers.

"What are your names?" asked one of the king's men. Mulan's new friends gave their names, and the man wrote them in a book. Mulan gave the man her father's name.

"You're all the king's soldiers now," said the soldier. "You'll sleep here tonight."

Mulan was now one soldier in an **army** of thousands of men.

"I'm a woman, but nobody knows," she thought. She slept very well that night.

The next day, the soldiers rode across the country and met their **enemies**. They fought for many days and each day Mulan was very brave. After some weeks she was a **general**. She rode in front of hundreds of men, and she fought **bravely**.

One day, there was a big fight with an enemy army. Mulan saw one of her soldiers with twelve enemy soldiers near him. The soldier had to fight the men, and Mulan wanted to help him. She rode her horse, and she came near to her soldier and his enemies. Mulan fought the enemies bravely, and then pulled her soldier up on her horse.

In the next twelve years, Mulan did a lot of brave things. The soldiers loved her, but they did not know her secret.

At home, Mulan's sister had no news from Mulan. "Is she dead?" she thought. "Or do they know her secret now?"

Then the war ended and the enemy army left. Mulan went to see the king.

"Thank you, general," said the king. "You fought well, and you killed many enemies. What do you want now? You can stay with me and you'll be the general of all my armies. You'll be a rich and famous man."

"Thank you," said Mulan. "But I only want one thing. Can I have a good horse? I want to go home to my village."

"Do you only want a horse?" asked the king. "Do you want anything more?"

"I want to see my family," said Mulan. "I don't want anything more."

The king gave Mulan a fine horse and she rode back to her village. Her parents had grey hair now, and her little sister was a woman.

"I'm home," said Mulan. She took off her father's armour, and wore her women's clothes. Her father and mother were very happy.

"Thank you, Mulan," said her father. He took his sword from her. "You were a very brave woman. We'll have a big dinner for all the village. And you must tell us stories about the wars and the fighting."

After six months, some soldiers came to visit their old general. Mulan came out of the house in women's clothes and make-up.

"Hello," she said. "I'm Mulan, and I was your general. Now I'm at home, and I don't need my armour."

The soldiers looked at her. Their mouths were open. "You were a wonderful general," they laughed. "But we never knew your great secret!"

Hanuman the fighter –
a story from India

Sugriva, the Monkey King, watched two young men. They walked bravely, and they had fine swords. But they wore old clothes, and they were very tired. What did they want? And why were they in Kishkindha, the country of the monkeys?

"Hanuman," said Sugriva to his friend. "Can you change into a man? Go and talk to them. What do they want?"

Hanuman changed from a monkey into a poor man in old clothes. He walked up to the two men.

"Who are you?" Hanuman asked. "You have fine clothes, but they are old. Are you kings or poor men? Why are you here in Kishkindha?"

"I am Rama," said one of the men. "And this is my younger brother Lakshmana. We are **hunting** the bad king Ravana. He has my wife, Sita. She is his **prisoner**."

"These are good men," thought Hanuman. "And I want to help them. King Ravana is a **terrible** man. The gods are frightened of him because he is a demon with ten heads and twenty arms."

"Can you help King Sugriva first?" asked Hanuman. "Then we can help you to find your wife. I am Hanuman, and I have many powers." Hanuman was now a monkey again.

"What can we do for you?" asked Rama.

"Sugriva is fighting his brother's army," said Hanuman. "Help Sugriva first, and then you can use his army. The monkeys fight well, and they can help you."

Rama and Lakshmana fought with Sugriva's army. Then Sugriva's brother ran away.

Now Sugriva's armies could help Rama. Across the country, millions of monkeys looked for Sita. After many days they came to a great sea.

A bird flew over the sea. "Across this sea is Lanka, the

country of demons," said the bird. "I saw Ravana. He took a woman to Lanka. She was very beautiful."

"The woman was Sita," said Rama.

"But how do we cross the sea?" asked the monkeys.

"My father is god of the wind," said Hanuman. "I can jump across the sea to Lanka!"

His body grew bigger and bigger, and his tail grew longer and longer. Now Hanuman was taller than a tree. He **climbed** to the top of a high **mountain**, and he jumped across the sea.

Then a terrible demon jumped up out of the water! It took Hanuman's tail in his mouth and tried to eat him. Hanuman killed the demon. He went across the sea again, and he came to Lanka.

Hanuman saw the lights of the demons' city. He changed again. He was now a very small animal, and he looked everywhere for Sita. After many hours he found her and changed into a monkey again.

Sita was Ravana's prisoner, and she was very sad. "Why are you here, monkey?" she asked.

"I am here for your husband Rama," said Hanuman. "I have this ring from him."

"Is Rama coming for me?" asked Sita.

"He will come in a day or two," said Hanuman.

Hanuman went outside, and he grew very big again. He started to **destroy** the trees and the buildings in the city. The demons fought Hanuman, but he killed them easily.

"I am Hanuman!" he shouted. "I am the son of the wind. I kill my enemies, and I fight for Rama. Ravana, you must give Sita to me or I will destroy your city."

"Never," shouted Ravana. Then he said to his demons, "Kill this monkey!"

The demons started a fire on Hanuman's tail, but he laughed. He moved his tail and then the fire was on all the buildings in Lanka.

"I'll be back," he shouted to Ravana. "And you'll be sorry!"

Then he jumped back across the sea. He put his tail in the sea and stopped the fire.

"Sita is in Lanka," Hanuman told Rama. "I talked to her and she's fine. And we can fight Ravana now. I killed a lot of demons and many buildings are burning. Lanka's armies cannot fight us."

"Then we must cross the sea and find Sita!" said Rama.

"And we must destroy the terrible demon Ravana!" said Lakshmana.

The monkey army destroyed many mountains, and they pushed them down into the sea. They made a road, and they walked across the sea to Lanka with Rama and Lakshmana.

The demons were ready and the two armies started to fight.

"I'm dying!" shouted Lakshmana.

Rama ran to his brother. "We need some special **herbs** from a mountain for Lakshmana," he said to Hanuman.

Hanuman jumped over the two armies and found a mountain. There were many different herbs on it. "What herb do I take for Lakshmana?" thought Hanuman. "I don't know. I'll take the mountain and the herbs."

Hanuman carried the mountain to Rama. Rama found the right herb and gave it to Lakshmana. Then Hanuman hit a demon with the mountain and killed it.

Ravana and Rama fought. But Rama had a special bow and arrow. One of his arrows hit Ravana and killed him. Then Ravana's army stopped fighting and ran away.

"Thank you for your good work," said Rama to Hanuman. "Can you give the good news to Sita?"

Hanuman smiled and ran. He wanted to find Sita. "Not bad for a monkey," he thought. "Not bad!"

Shahrazad the story-teller – a story from many places

Shahrazad was a very intelligent young woman. She lived with her younger sister, Dunyazad, and their father. Their father worked for the king.

One evening, Shahrazad went into the house. Her father sat by the fire with a very sad face.

"What's the matter, father?" she asked.

"I'm sad for you, my daughter," said her father and he started to cry. "I must tell you about our great king, Shahriyar. He had a beautiful wife, and he loved her. But one day, he came home and found his wife with another man. He called his soldiers. 'Kill her,' he said. '**Cut off** her head!' And the soldiers cut off her head. 'I'll marry again,' said the king. 'But I'll never again find my wife with another man. I'll marry on one day, and the next day my soldiers will kill my new wife. I'll have a new wife every day!'

"One day," said Shahrazad's father. "The king will want to marry you! And on the next day he'll cut off your head!"

"Don't cry, father," said Shahrazad.

"But I can't stop crying," said her father. "He'll marry you, and the soldiers will cut off your head. And then he'll marry your sister, and he'll kill her, too."

That night, Shahrazad did not sleep. She needed to think. She did not want to die, but there was something more important. "I don't want my sister, and many more women to die," she thought. "What can I do? How can I **save** the women of this country?"

It was now early in the morning, and the birds started to sing. "I know," thought Shahrazad. "I have a plan but it's not easy. I must be brave, but maybe I can do it."

At breakfast, Shahrazad told her father, "I'm ready to marry the king tomorrow."

"No," said Shahrazad's father. "Don't marry him tomorrow. I don't want you to die."

"It's all right, Father," said Shahrazad. "I have a secret plan. I will not die, and no more women will

die because of the king. I can save them. But please do one thing for me. In the middle of the night, at twelve o'clock, Dunyazad must come to me."

"She'll come," said her father. "But how can she help you? I don't understand."

Shahrazad did not answer. The next day, she married the king.

All that day, the king watched Shahrazad. "Why is she happy?" he thought. "She's going to die tomorrow. She knows that. I'm sorry because she's a fine, intelligent woman."

That night, the king and Shahrazad went to their bedroom. But at twelve o'clock someone came to the door.

"Who is that?" asked the king.

Dunyazad opened the bedroom door.

"I'm sorry," she said to the king. "I want to say goodbye to my sister."

She ran across the room to Shahrazad. "Sister," she said. "Can you finish the story of Aladdin first? Then I can say goodbye to you." She looked at the king and smiled. "Please! Is that all right?"

"All right," said the king, but he was not happy.

But, after a few minutes, the king started to listen to the story because Shahrazad was a great story-teller.

After an hour, Shahrazad finished. "Do you know any more stories?" asked the king.

"Yes," said Shahrazad. She started to tell the story of Sindbad. Sindbad travelled in his ship to many different countries. The story was good, and it got better and better. The king listened, but then Shahrazad stopped.

"I'm sorry," she said. "I'm very tired." And she lay down on the bed. She went to sleep and Dunyazad went home.

The next morning, the king's soldiers came to the door. They were ready to cut off Shahrazad's head.

"Not today," said the king. "I want to hear the end of the story of Sindbad. Come for my wife tomorrow!"

"What happens to Sindbad in the story?" thought the king. He thought about it all day. "I must know the end of the story!"

Shahrazad finished the story that night.

"That was a good story," said the king. "I learned a lot from Sindbad. He was very brave and intelligent. I want to be the same!"

"You are brave and intelligent," said Shahrazad. "But you can learn more from the story of Ali Baba."

"Tell me the story," said the king.

"Not now," said Shahrazad. "I'm tired. I want to sleep."

The next morning, the soldiers came to the door again. "Go away!" said the king. And he said it again, one thousand times. Each night, there was a new story from Shahrazad.

On night 1,001, the king asked for another story.

Shahrazad was sad. "I'm sorry. I don't have any more stories," she said. "I told you all the stories in the books in my father's **library**. I can't tell any more."

"I loved your stories," the king told Shahrazad. "And now I will give you one thing. What do you want? You can ask for anything."

"You can cut off my head," said Shahrazad. "But please don't kill any more women after me. There are many good women in this country, and they must live."

"You must live, too," said the king. "You're a brave and intelligent woman. I want you next to me. A king needs a friend, and you can help me."

King Shahriyar and Queen Shahrazad lived together for many years.

Shahriyar was a better king because of Shahrazad. They had a baby, and the king built a library for all the people in his country. Because stories are for everyone.

Anansi the spider-man –
a story from Ghana

There were no stories in the world. Nobody could tell any stories. Anansi, son of the sky god, did not know any stories. Nyame was Anansi's father. He had all the stories, but they were in a big box. Nyame had the key to his box, and he did not give the key to anyone.

Anansi looked at the world, and he talked to his wife, Aso. "The world is a very sad place," he said. "We need stories. With stories, children will laugh every day."

"You can change. You can be a spider and talk to your father," said Aso. "He has the stories. He must open his box."

Anansi changed into a spider, and he climbed up to the sky. He went to see his father, Nyame.

"Open your box, father," said Anansi. "Give the stories to the world."

Nyame laughed. "You can't have something for nothing, my son. Bring me three things and you can have my box."

"What three things do you want?" asked Anansi.

"I want the great snake, Onini," said Nyame. "I want the Mmoboro hornets, and I want Osebo the leopard. Bring me those things and you can have all the stories."

"I'll bring you those three things," said Anansi. "That's not a problem!"

Anansi was a very intelligent spider, and his wife Aso was a very intelligent woman. They thought about a plan all night, and in the morning they were ready.

Anansi walked through the trees with a long stick. He was angry. "She's very stupid," he shouted. "She's wrong and I'm right!"

Onini the snake was up in a tree, and he heard Anansi. "Why are you angry?" he asked.

"It's my stupid wife," said Anansi. "'Onini is not a long snake,' she says. 'He's shorter than your stick, Anansi!' But is she right?"

"Of course I am longer than your stick!" said Onini.

He was angry now, too. He came down from the tree and lay next to the stick. He was nearly as long as the stick.

"I can **tie** your tail to the stick with my web," said Anansi. "Then I can pull you. You'll get longer."

Anansi tied Onini's tail to the stick with his web.

"The stick is a little longer than you," said Anansi.

"Tie my head to the stick with your web and pull again," said Onini.

Anansi tied the snake's head. Onini was now as long as the stick, but he could not move because of the web. Then Anansi carried Onini to his father.

"Good!" said Nyame. "But there are two more things."

"I know," said Anansi. "I'll get the hornets now!"

Anansi found a gourd and put water in it. He went to the hornets' nest and **poured** water into it from his gourd.

The hornets were very angry. They wanted to fight, but Anansi shouted, "It's raining. You must do something. Rain is not good for hornets."

"What can we do?" asked the hornets. "Where can we go?"

"You can go into my gourd," said Anansi. "The rain can't come in there."

The hornets flew into the gourd. Then Anansi made some more web, and he closed the gourd with it. The hornets were prisoners. Anansi carried the gourd and the hornets to his father.

"Here you are!" he said. "The Mmoboro hornets."

"That's very good," said his father. "Now I have two things, but I wanted three things. And Osebo the leopard will be difficult."

"That's not a problem," said Anansi. "I don't like easy jobs!"

Anansi climbed down from the sky and went into the trees. Osebo liked to hunt there. Anansi made a big hole in the ground and put some web over it. Then he put some leaves and sticks on the web. You could not see the hole.

Anansi sat in a tree near the hole, and he waited for Osebo.

In the evening, Anansi heard a loud noise. Osebo was in the hole.

"Help me!" shouted Osebo.

"I can help you," said Anansi. "Wait a minute!"

Anansi took a long green tree, and pushed the top of the tree down into the hole. Then he took some web and gave it to Osebo. "Tie this web to the tree and to your tail," he said.

Osebo took the web and tied his tail to the top of the tree. Then Anansi **let go** of the tree and the leopard flew up into the sky. Nyame was in his home in the sky and Osebo stopped at his feet. Anansi watched Osebo, and then climbed up to the sky on his web.

Nyame laughed. Then he went to his room and found his beautiful box. Nyame and Anansi listened to it, and they could hear noises inside. They were the noises of all the stories.

"Here you are," said Nyame. "You worked hard, and you can have my box of stories and the key."

Anansi took the box. Then he put this story about Anansi and the snake, the hornets and the leopard into the box with the others. He went home with the box and showed it to Aso.

At home, Aso was very happy. "We have the box!" she said. Anansi and Aso opened the box. All the stories came out and flew across the world. The children laughed at the stories. Their parents loved the stories, too. Now the world was a happier place.

During-reading questions

1 Why do Hua and his wife call their baby Mulan?
2 Mulan's father can't go to war. Why not?
3 Mulan has to change to be a soldier. How does she do that?
4 Whose name does Mulan give to the king's man?
5 After the war, what two things does Mulan want from the king?
6 Who visits Mulan at her home? What do they learn about her?

HANUMAN THE FIGHTER – A STORY FROM INDIA

1 Why does Rama come to the country of the monkeys?
2 Where does Ravana take Sita?
3 How does Hanuman go across the sea?
4 How does the monkey army go across the sea?
5 What does Hanuman carry to Rama? Why does he do that?
6 How does Rama stop the fighting?

SHAHRAZAD THE STORY-TELLER –
A STORY FROM MANY PLACES

1 Why is Shahrazad's father unhappy?
2 Shahrazad does not sleep one night. Why?
3 Who comes to the king's bedroom door at twelve o'clock?
4 What does Dunyazad want Shahrazad to do?
5 Shahrazad tells a second story. What is it?
6 Shahrazad cannot tell the story of Ali Baba. Why?
7 Shahrazad wants one thing from the king. What does she ask?
8 What does the king build for his people? Why?

1 Where are all the stories in the world?
2 What does Anansi want Nyame to do?
3 What three things does Nyame want from Anansi?
4 How does Anansi bring Onini to Nyame?
5 How does Anansi bring the Mmoboro hornets to Nyame?
6 What do Anansi and Aso do with the box?

After-reading questions

1 Mulan does not want the other soldiers to know her secret. Why is that, do you think?

2 Mulan says: "I can fight with one hand behind my back." Why does she say that?

3 At the end of his story Hanuman says, "Not bad for a monkey." Why does he say that?

4 The king kills many women, but Shahrazad marries him. Why does she marry him?

5 What are Shahrazad's first three stories? Do you know them?

6 Do stories make people happy? What do you think?

Exercises

1 Write the correct word in your notebook. Then write
sentences in your notebook.

1 erpow ..... *power* ..... *Mulan's special power is fighting.*

2 bvare ....

3 rwa ....

4 resetc ....

5 kmae-pu ....

6 yram ....

7 ymene ....

8 relagen ....

2 Complete these sentences in your notebook with the
correct form of the verb.

Hua put a tree in his garden and it [1]........ *grew* .... (**grow**) tall.
Mulan [2]........... (**be**) wonderful with horses, and she [3]...........
(**learn**) to fight with a sword. Mulan [4].......... (**put**) her long hair
on top of her head and [5]........... (**take**) off her make-up. Mulan [6]
.... (**ride**) away from the village on her best horse. She [7]...........
(**meet**) some men from other villages. "I'm a woman, but
nobody knows," she [8]........... (**think**).

3 **Are these sentences *true* or *false*? Write the correct answers in your notebook.**

1 Rama and Lakshmana have fine clothes. ....*false*............
2 Rama and Lakshmana are hunting Sugriva the Monkey King.
3 Ravana is a demon with many heads and arms.
4 Sita is in the land of demons.
5 Hanuman swims to Lanka.
6 Hanuman gives Sita a sword.
7 The demons start a fire on Hanuman's tail.
8 Hanuman kills a demon with a sword.

4 **Complete these sentences in your notebook, using the words from the box.**

mountain	terrible	destroys	hunting	swords
	army	prisoner	herb	

1 Rama and his brother are ....*hunting*........ Ravana.
2 Sita is a .... in Lanka.
3 Rama and Lakshmana have fine ....
4 Ravana is a .... demon.
5 Sugriva's .... helps Rama and Lakshmana.
6 Hanuman jumps from a high ....
7 Hanuman .... the trees and buildings of the demons' city.
8 Hanuman finds a special .... for Lakshmana.

5 Write the correct question word. Then answer the questions in your notebook.

Who	When (x2)	What (x2)	How many	Where

1 ....*Where*........ did Shahrazad's father sit with a sad face?
He sat by the fire with a sad face.
2 .... did not sleep that night?
3 .... must Dunyazad come to Shahrazad?
4 .... story did Dunyazad want to hear?
5 .... did the soldiers come to the door?
6 .... stories did Shahrazad tell?
7 .... did the king build for all the people in his country?

6 Match the two parts of the sentences in your notebook.
Example: 1 – e

1 I'll marry on one day,
2 It was now early in the morning,
3 I must be brave,
4 In the middle of the night,
5 Can you finish
6 The story was good,
7 You can learn more
8 A king needs a friend,

a Dunyazad must come to me.
b and it got better and better.
c and the birds started to sing.
d from the story of Ali Baba.
e and the next day my soldiers will kill my new wife.
f the story of Aladdin first?
g and you can help me.
h but maybe I can do it.

7 **Put these sentences in the correct order in your notebook.**

a .... Anansi and Aso open the box of stories.

b .... Anansi and Aso think of a plan.

c .... Anansi pours water into the hornets' nest.

d .... Anansi takes the hornets to Nyame.

e ...*1*.... Anansi talks to his father about the box of stories.

f .... Anansi ties Onini to a stick.

g .... Nyame asks Anansi for three things.

h .... Osebo the leopard stops at Nyame's feet.

8 **Complete these sentences in your notebook, using the prepositions from the box.**

in	from	with	on	into
	about	up	over	

1 All the stories were ....*in*........... a big box.

2 Anansi changed .... a spider.

3 Anansi and Aso thought .... a plan all night, and in the morning they were ready.

4 Onini came down .... the tree and lay next to the stick.

5 Anansi made a big hole in the ground and put some web .... it.

6 Then he put some leaves and sticks .... the web.

7 Anansi let go of the tree and the leopard flew .... into the sky.

8 Anansi went home .... the box and showed it to Aso.

9 **Who says or thinks this? Write the correct answers in your notebook.**

1 "Maybe you will need to fight one day."
   Mulan's father, Hua..

2 "The important thing is inside me."

3 "The monkeys fight well, and they can help you."

4 "We must cross the sea and find Sita!"

5 "How can I save the women of this country?"

6 "Do you know any more stories?"

7 "You can't have something for nothing, my son."

8 "You can go into my gourd."

Project work

1 You are Mulan. Write a letter to your sister from the king's army. What are you doing, and how do you feel?

2 You are Rama. Write a note to Sita for Hanuman to take with the ring on his journey to Lanka.

3 In three nights, Shahrazad told three stories to the king. Choose one of the stories and learn about it. Then write the story.

4 One day, Nyame asks Anansi to bring him a monkey. How can Anansi do that? Write the story.

5 Make a poster about one of the four heroes.

6 Choose another hero. It could be someone from your country. Write their story or draw a picture story about them.

An answer key for all questions and exercises can be found at **www.penguinreaders.co.uk**

Glossary

army (n.)
a large group of soldiers (= soldiers fight for their country)

brave (adj.); **bravely** (adv.)
A *brave* person is not frightened. *Brave* people do things *bravely*.

climb (v.)
to use your hands and feet and move up, over, down or across something

cut off (phr. v.)
to cut through a part of something. Then that part is not there any more.

destroy (v.)
You *destroy* something and then it cannot live or you cannot use it.

enemy (n.)
You are fighting a person, group or country in a *war*. This person, group or country is your *enemy*.

general (n.)
an important person in an *army*

god (n.)
an important thing with special *powers*. You cannot see a *god*. In some stories, there are *gods* for many different things, for example, the sun, the rain and different animals.

herb (n.)
Herbs are plants (= things that grow). People use *herbs* for cooking and to make people or animals better if they are not well.

hunt (v.)
to look for someone or something. You also *hunt* for animals.

let go (phr. v.)
to stop holding something

library (n.)
There are a lot of books in a *library*. People can take a book, then bring it back.

make-up (n.)
colours for your face. Many women wear *make-up*.

mountain (n.)
A *mountain* is very high. People *climb mountains*.

pour (v.)
to put liquid (= a thing like water) into something

power (n.)
A person or a *god* has special *powers*.

prisoner (n.)
A *prisoner* cannot leave a place.

save (v.)
A person does not die because
you help them. You *save* them.

secret (n.)
Only some people know about a
secret. Other people do not know
about it. You must not talk about
secrets.

take off (phr. v.)
(past tense *took off*)
You are wearing *make-up*. You
take it *off*. Then you are not
wearing *make-up* any more.

terrible (adj.)
very bad

tie (v.)
to put a long, strong thing (in
this story it is a web) around
something. Then it cannot move.

war (n.)
fighting between countries or
groups of people